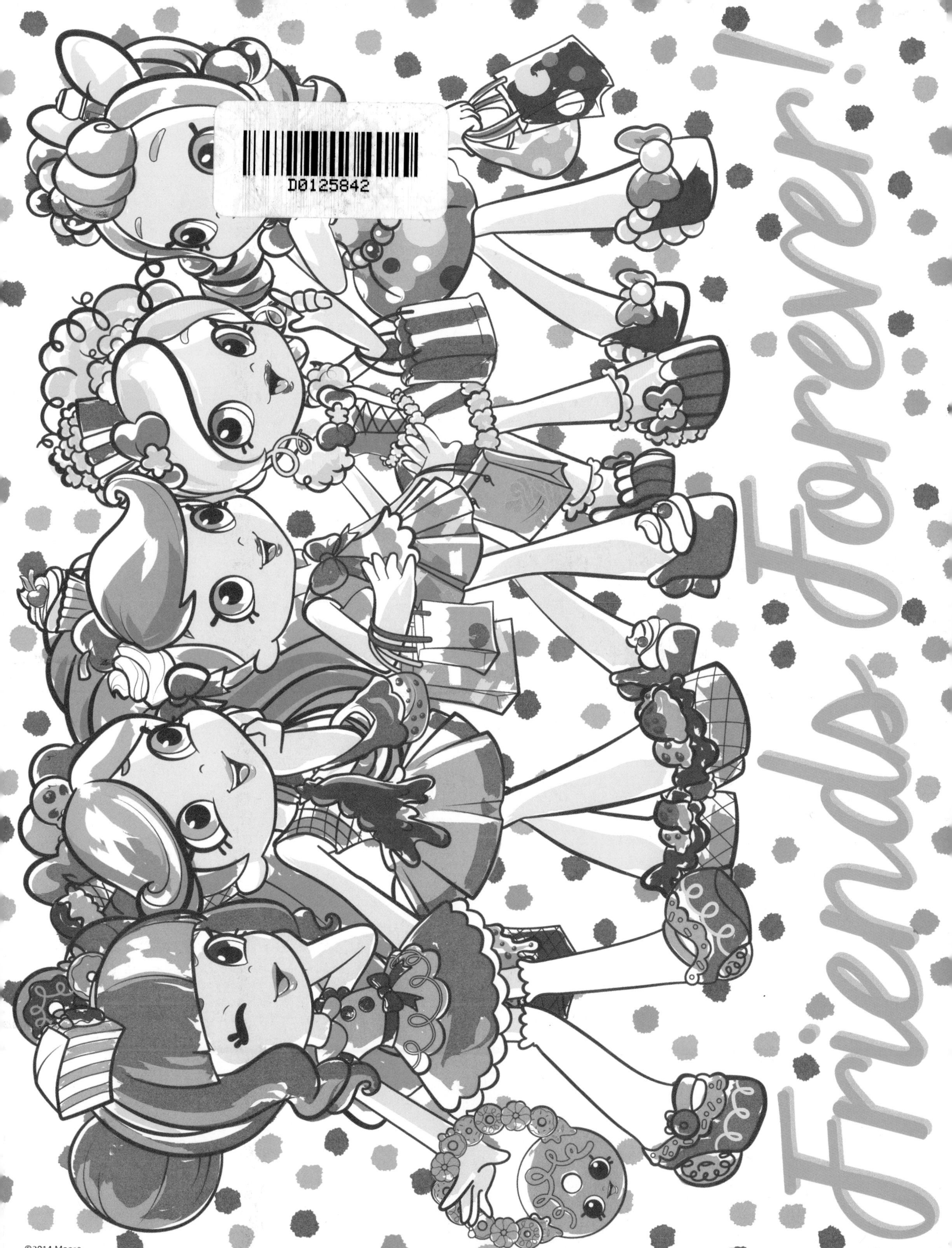
Friends Forever!

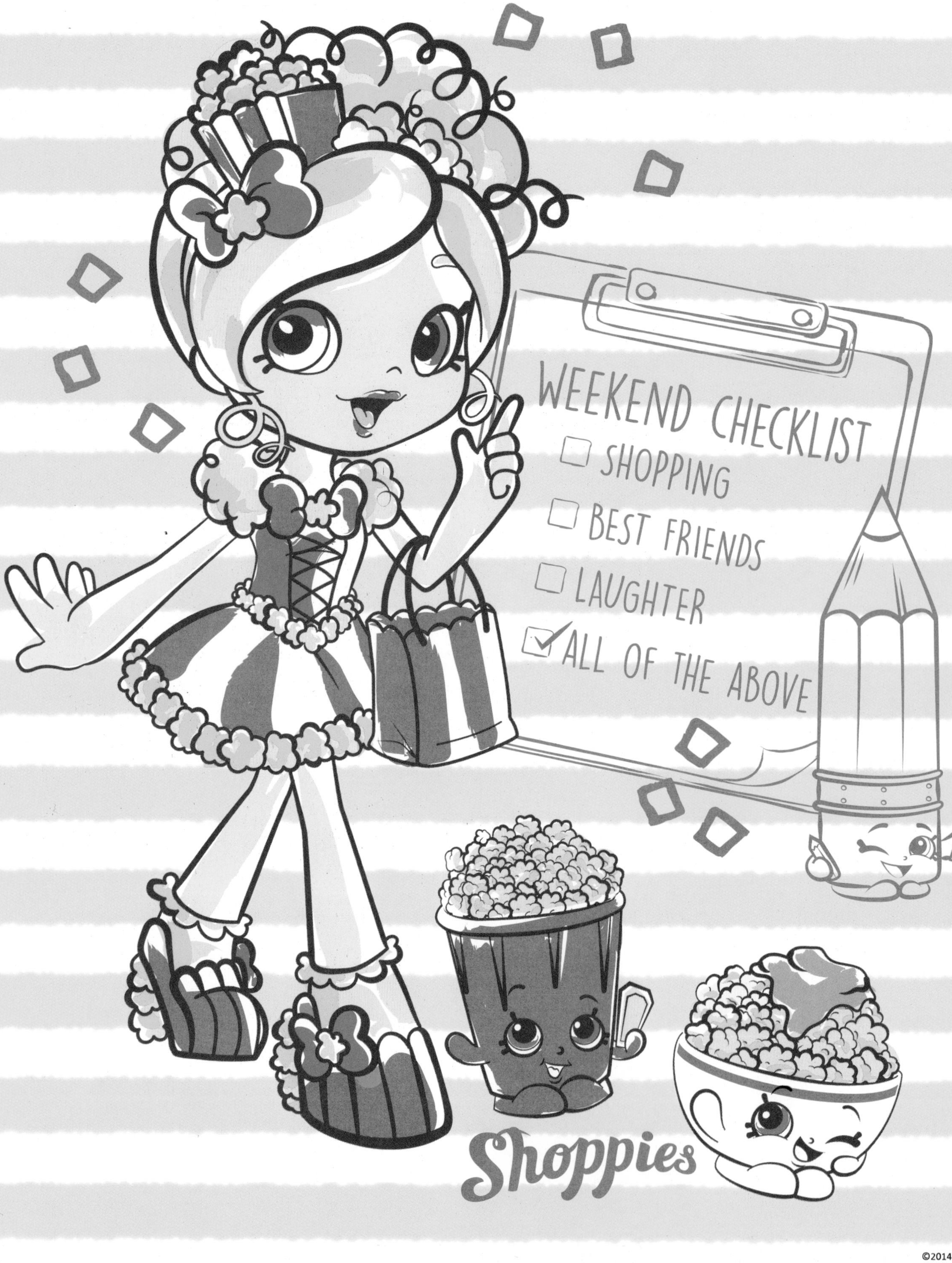
WEEKEND CHECKLIST
SHOPPING
BEST FRIENDS
LAUGHTER
ALL OF THE ABOVE
Shoppies

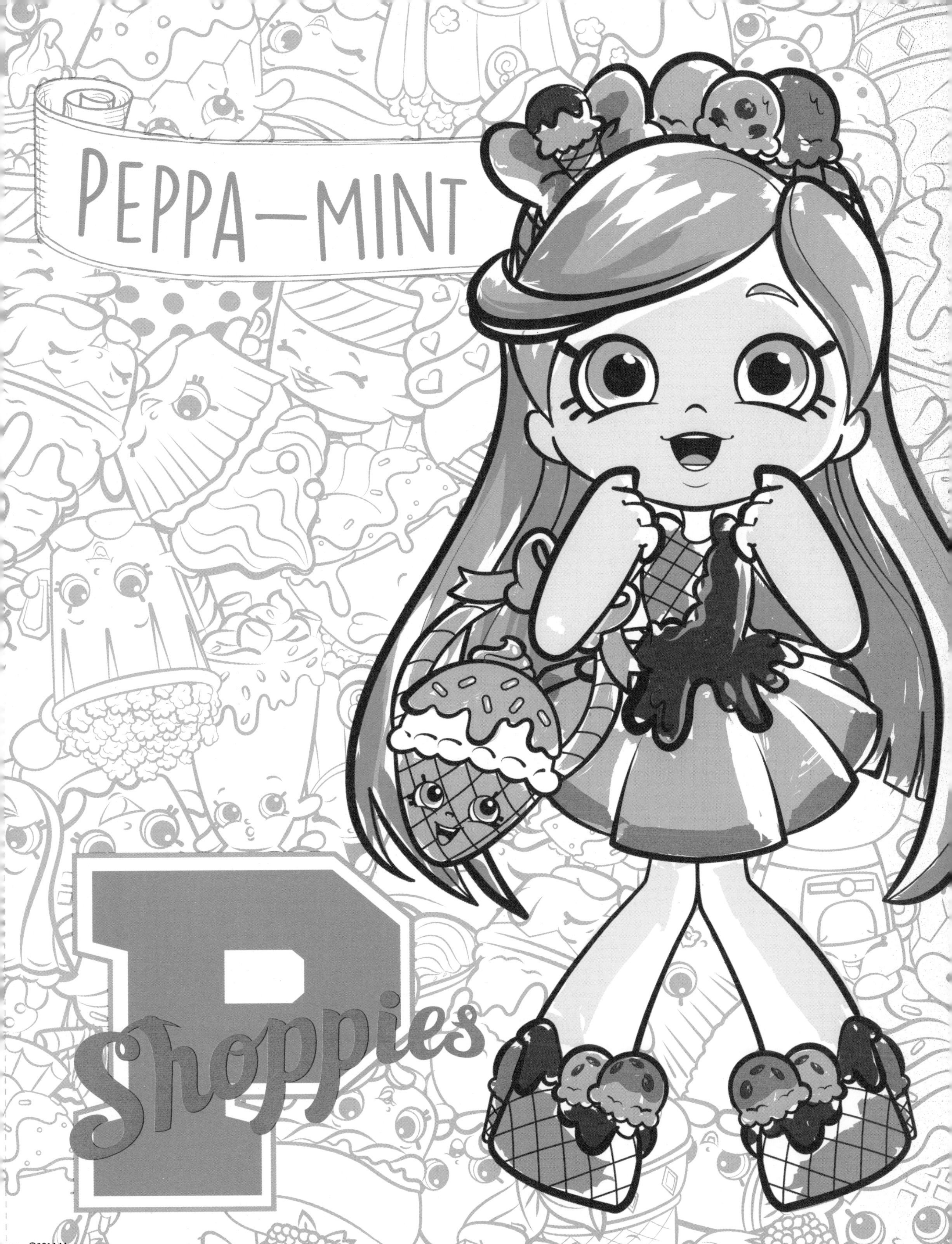
PEPPA-MINT
P
Shoppies

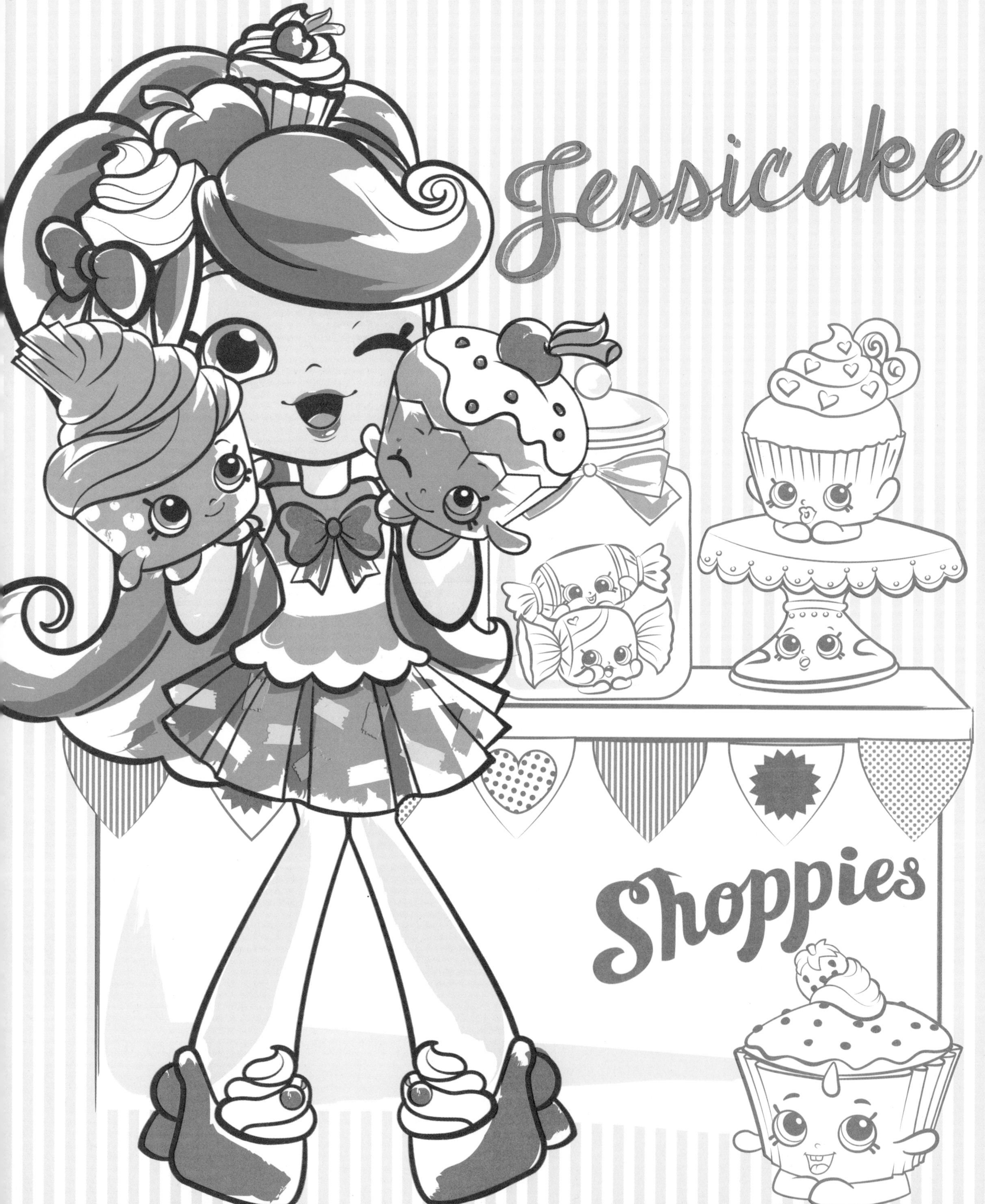
Jessicake
Shoppies

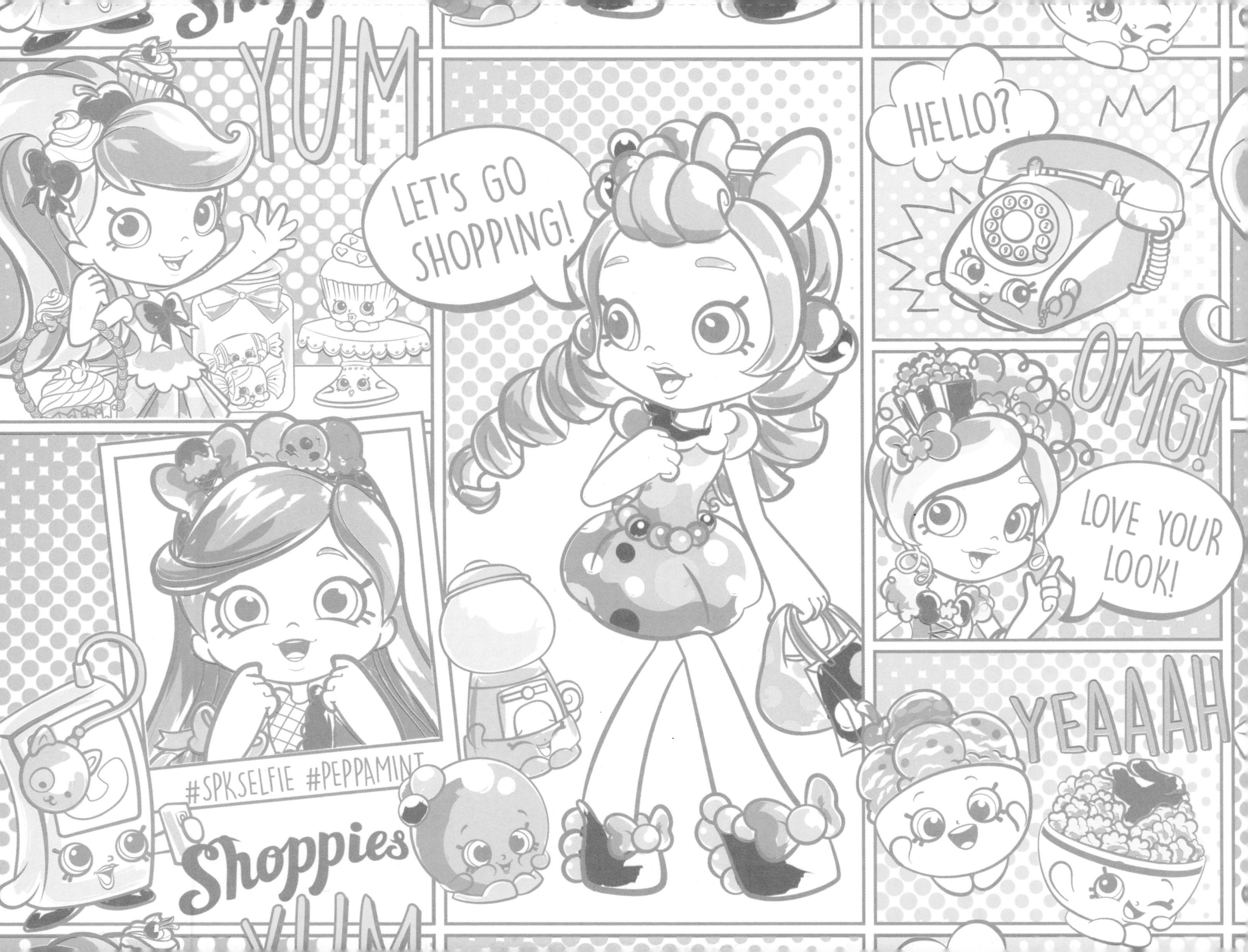
YUM
LET'S GO SHOPPING!
HELLO?
OMG!
LOVE YOUR LOOK!
YEAAAH
#SPKSELFIE #PEPPAMINT
Shoppies

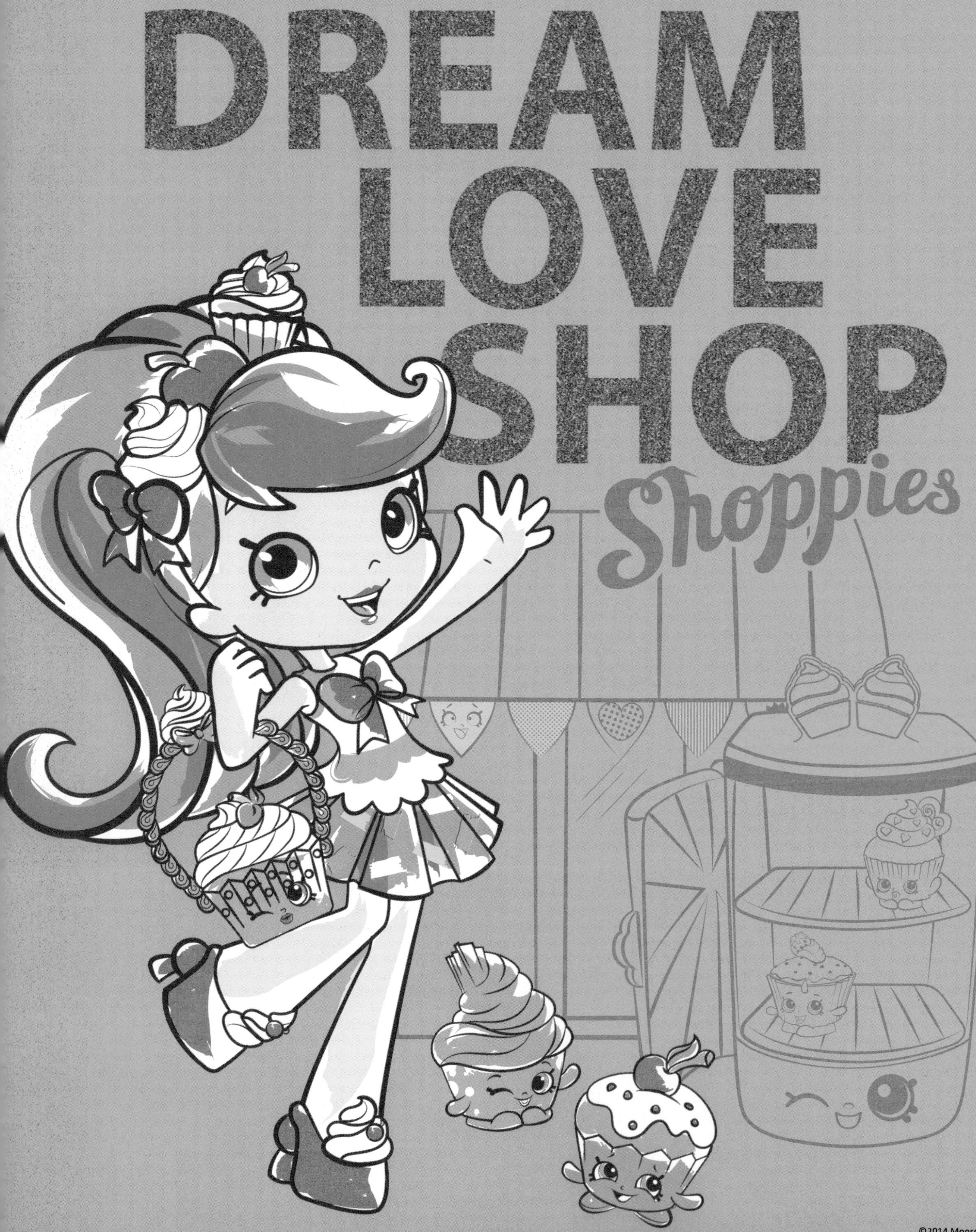
DREAM
LOVE
SHOP
Shoppies

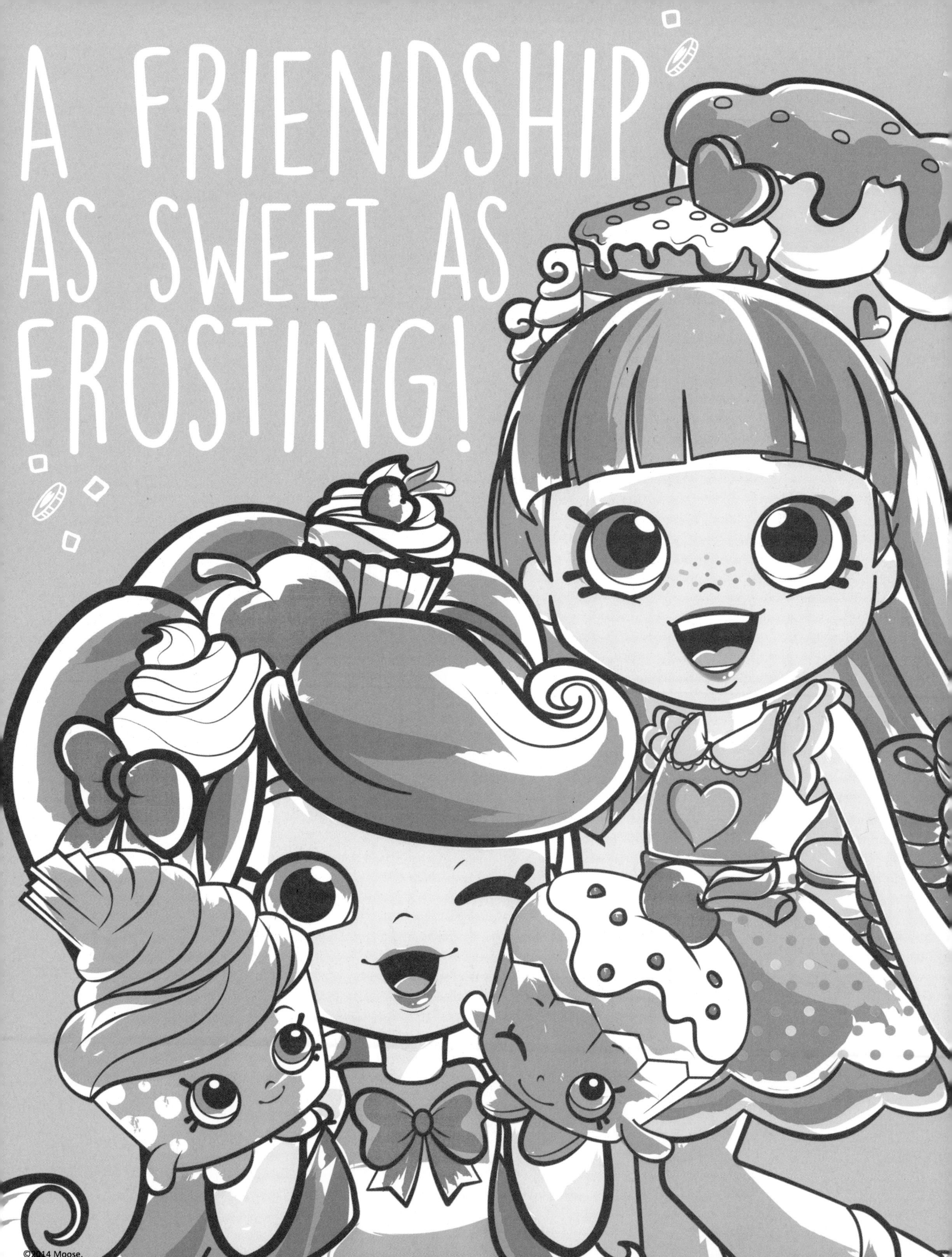
A FRIENDSHIP
AS SWEET AS
FROSTING!

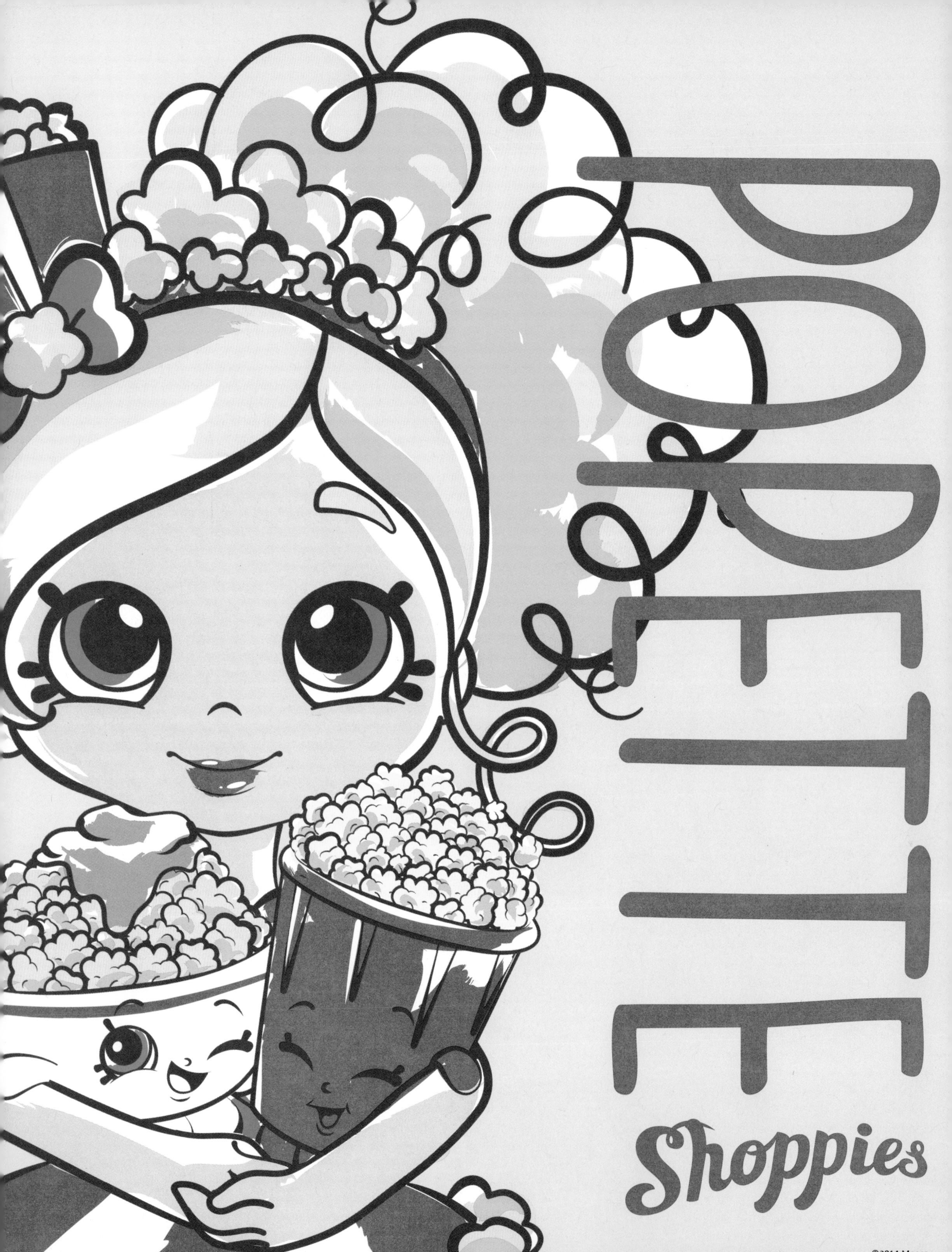
POPPETTE
Shoppies

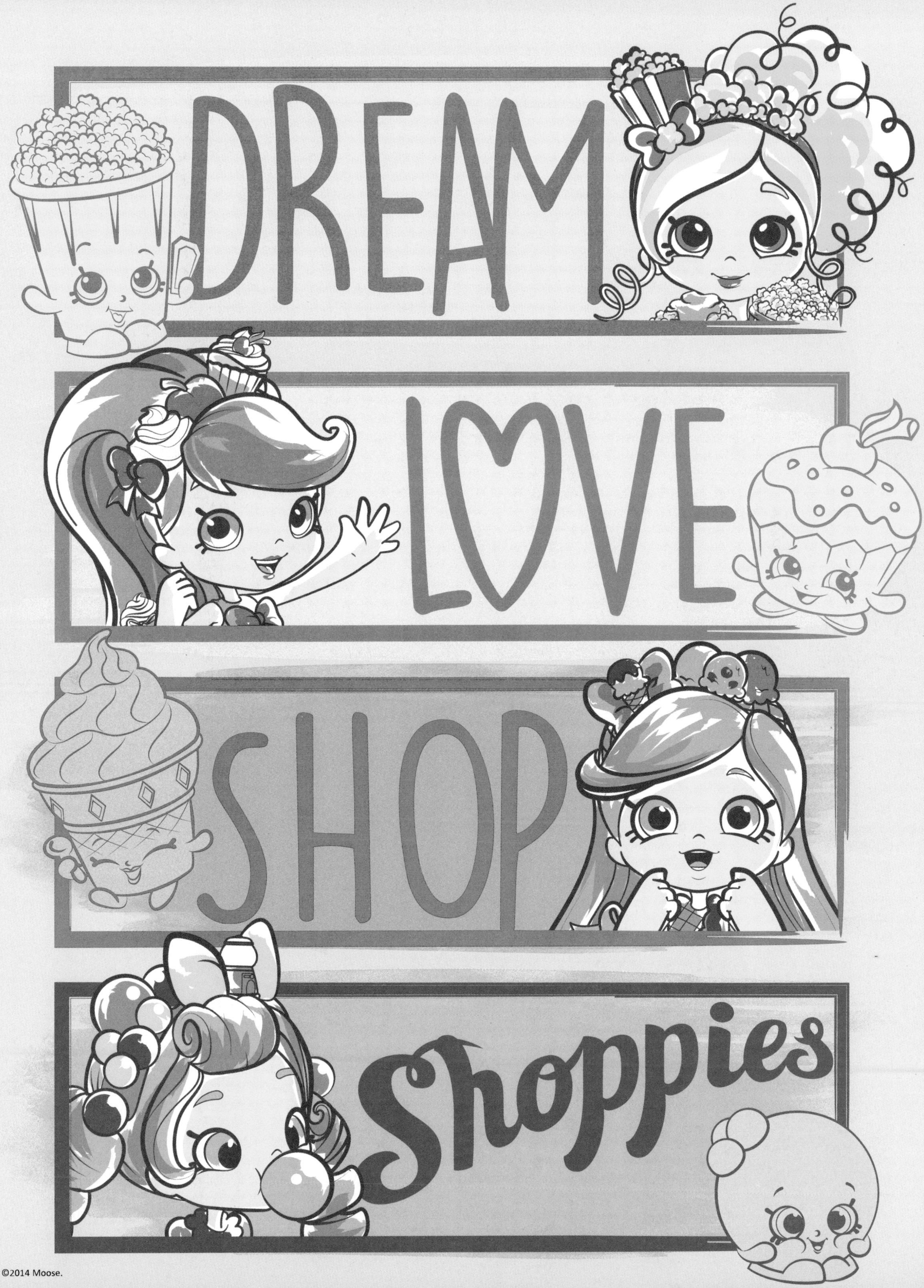
DREAM
LOVE
SHOP
Shoppies

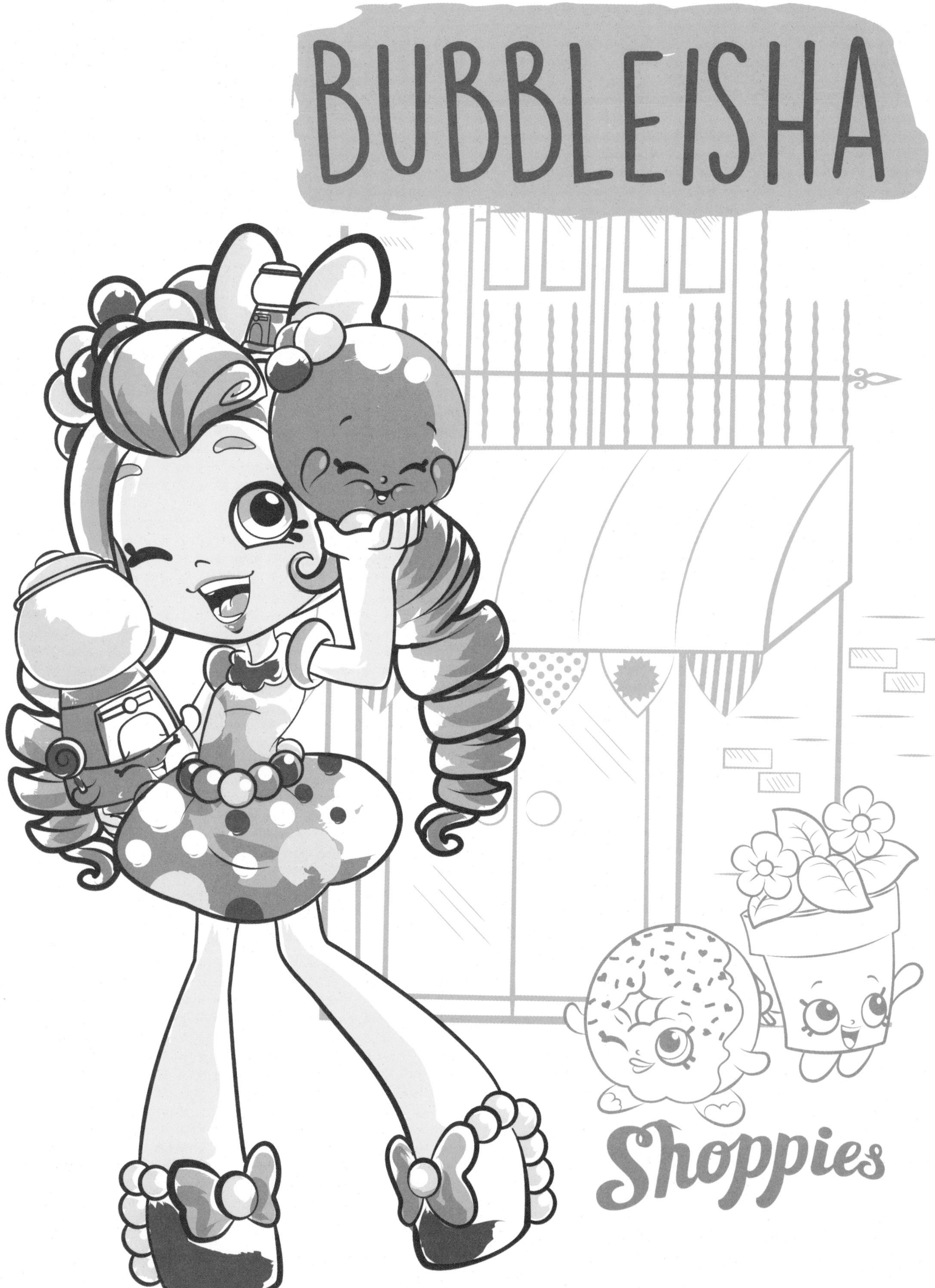
BUBBLEISHA
Shoppies

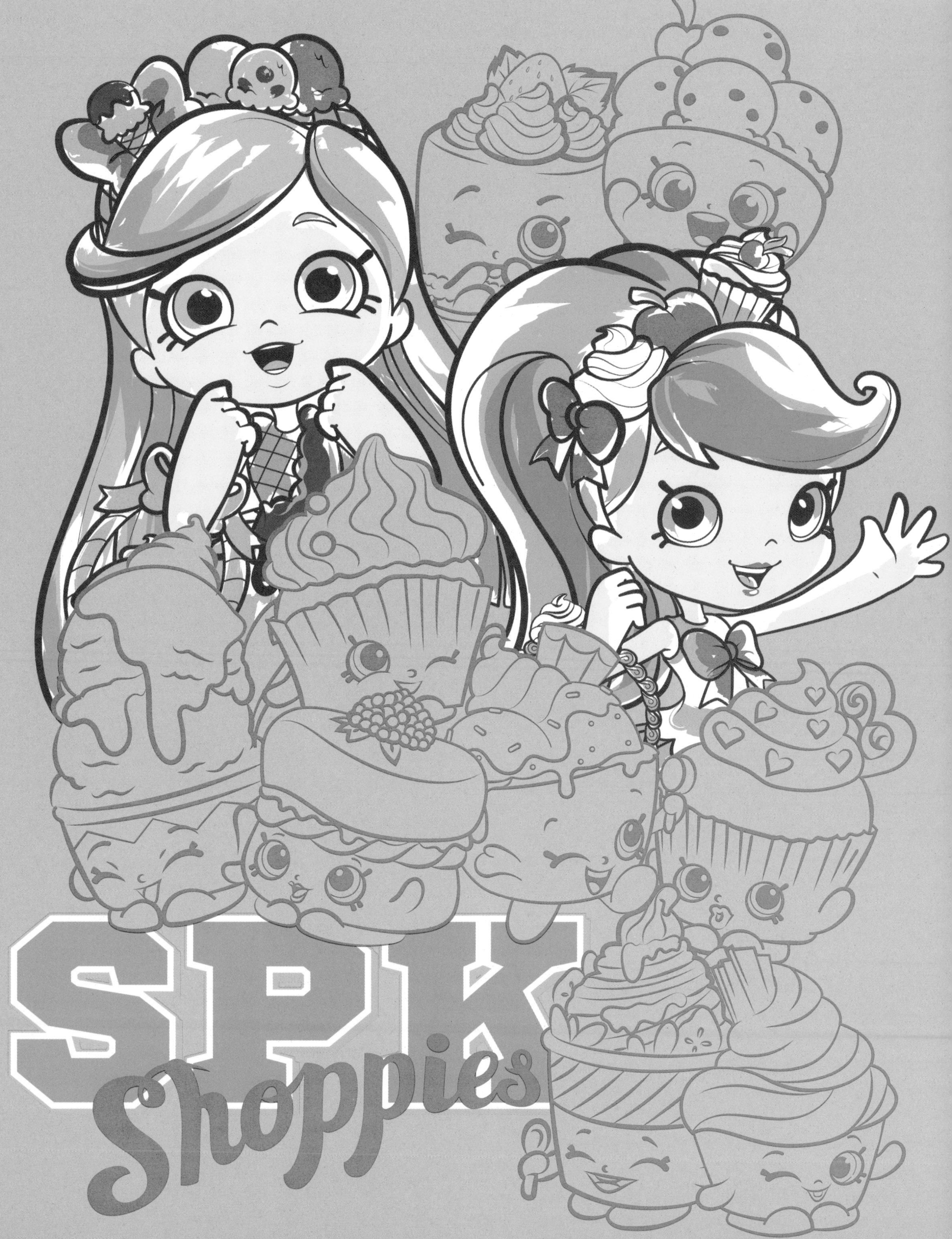
SPK
Shoppies

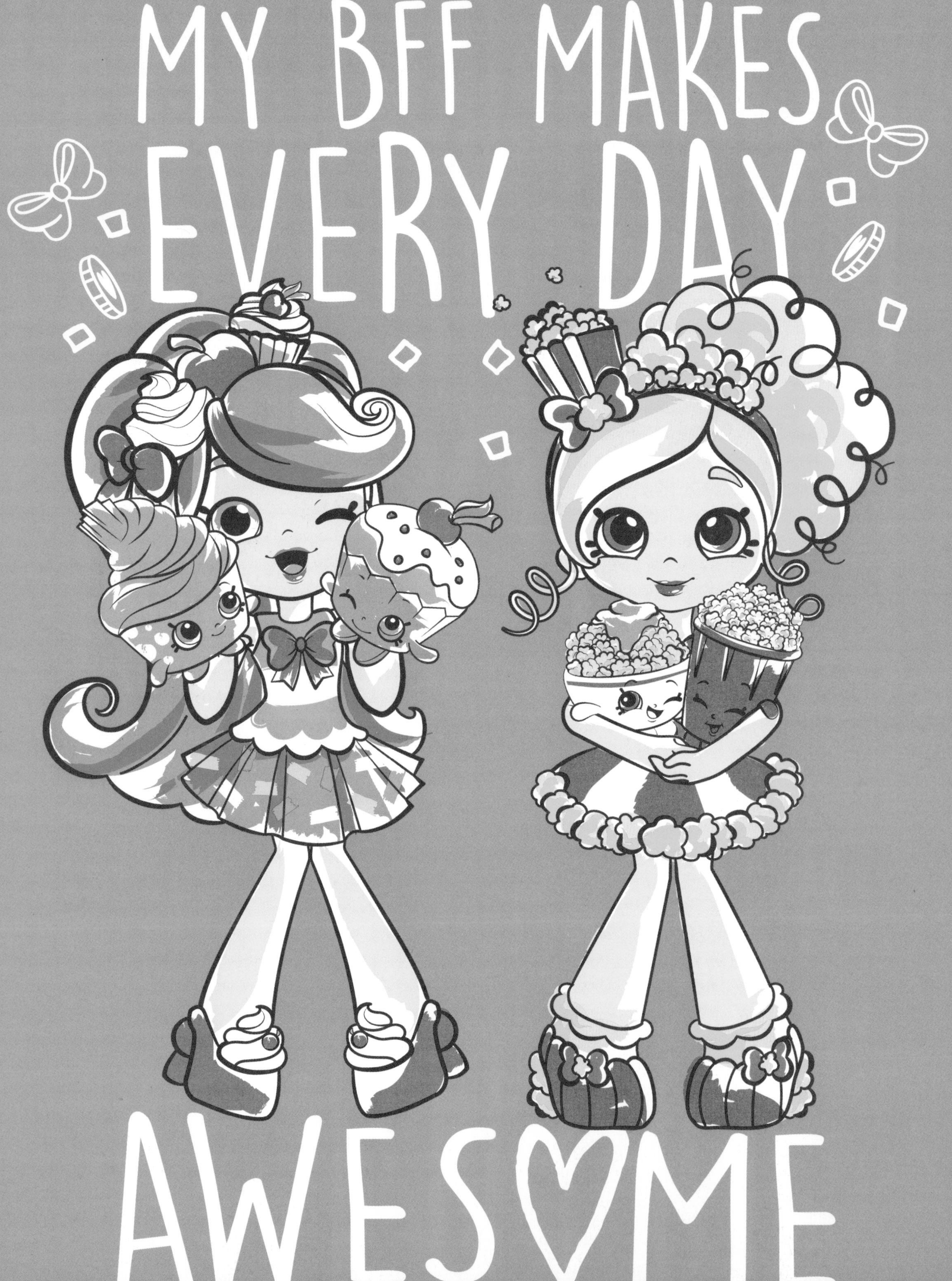
MY BFF MAKES
EVERY DAY
AWESOME

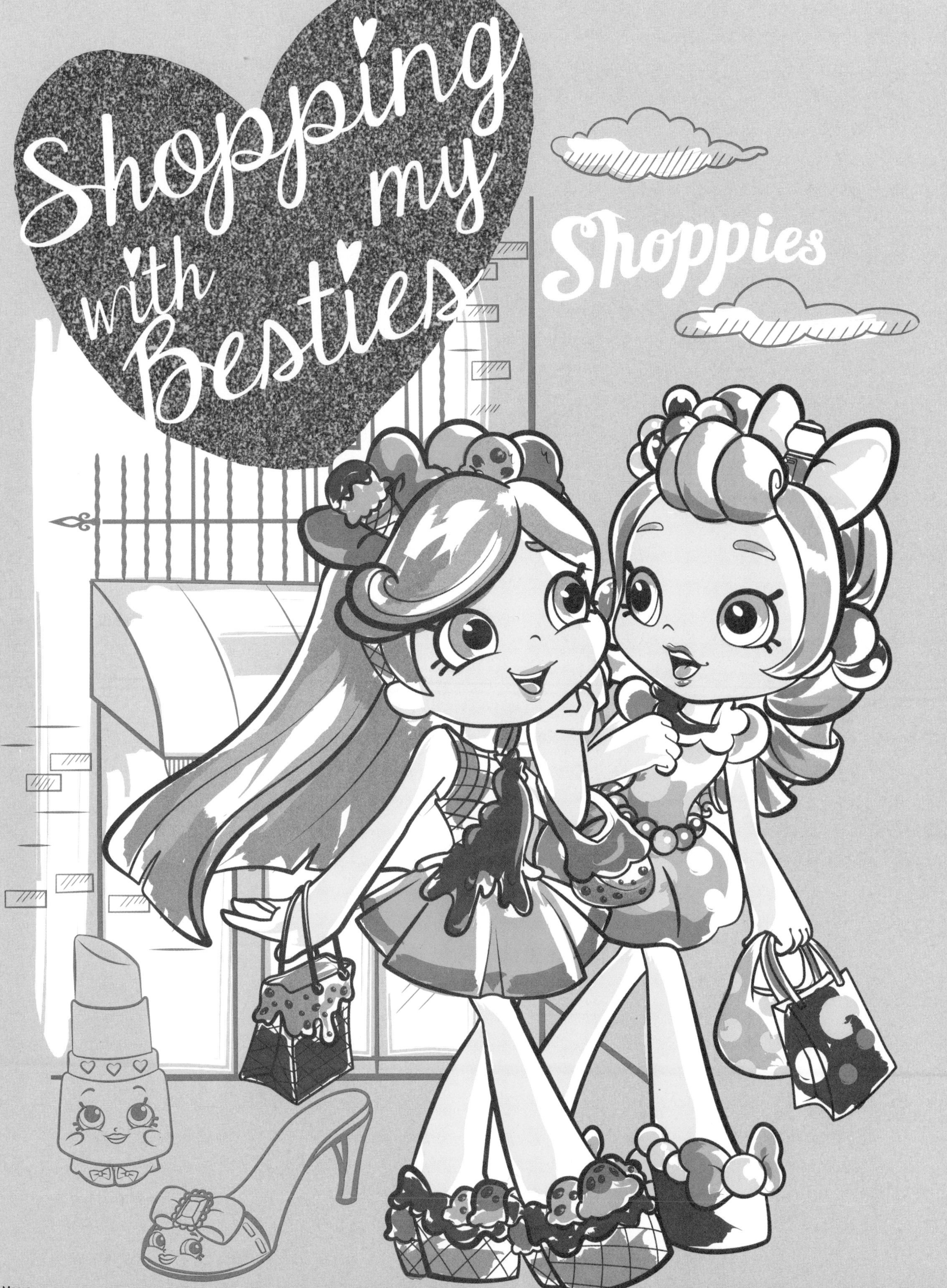
Shopping with my Besties
Shoppies

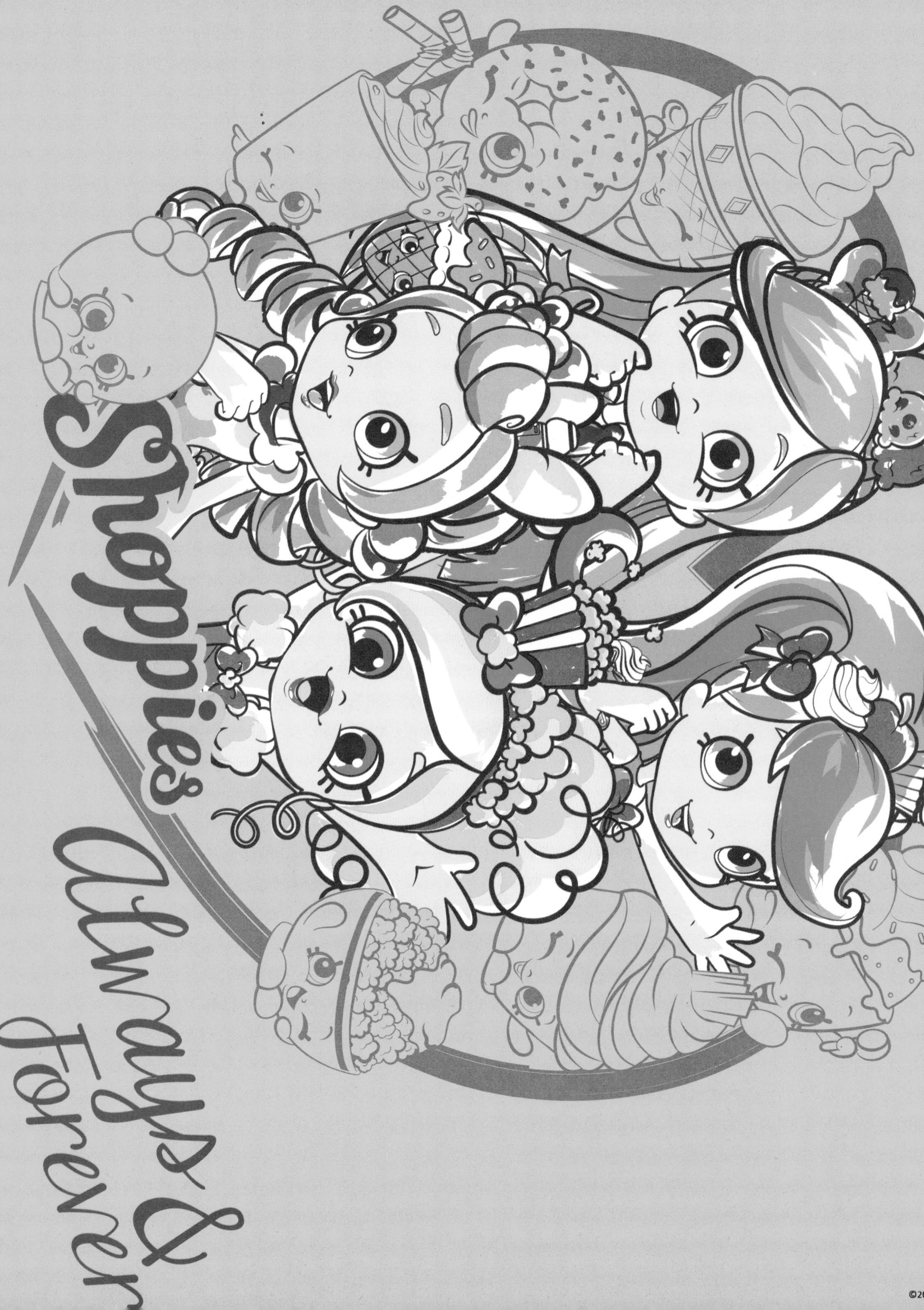
Shoppies
Always &
Forever

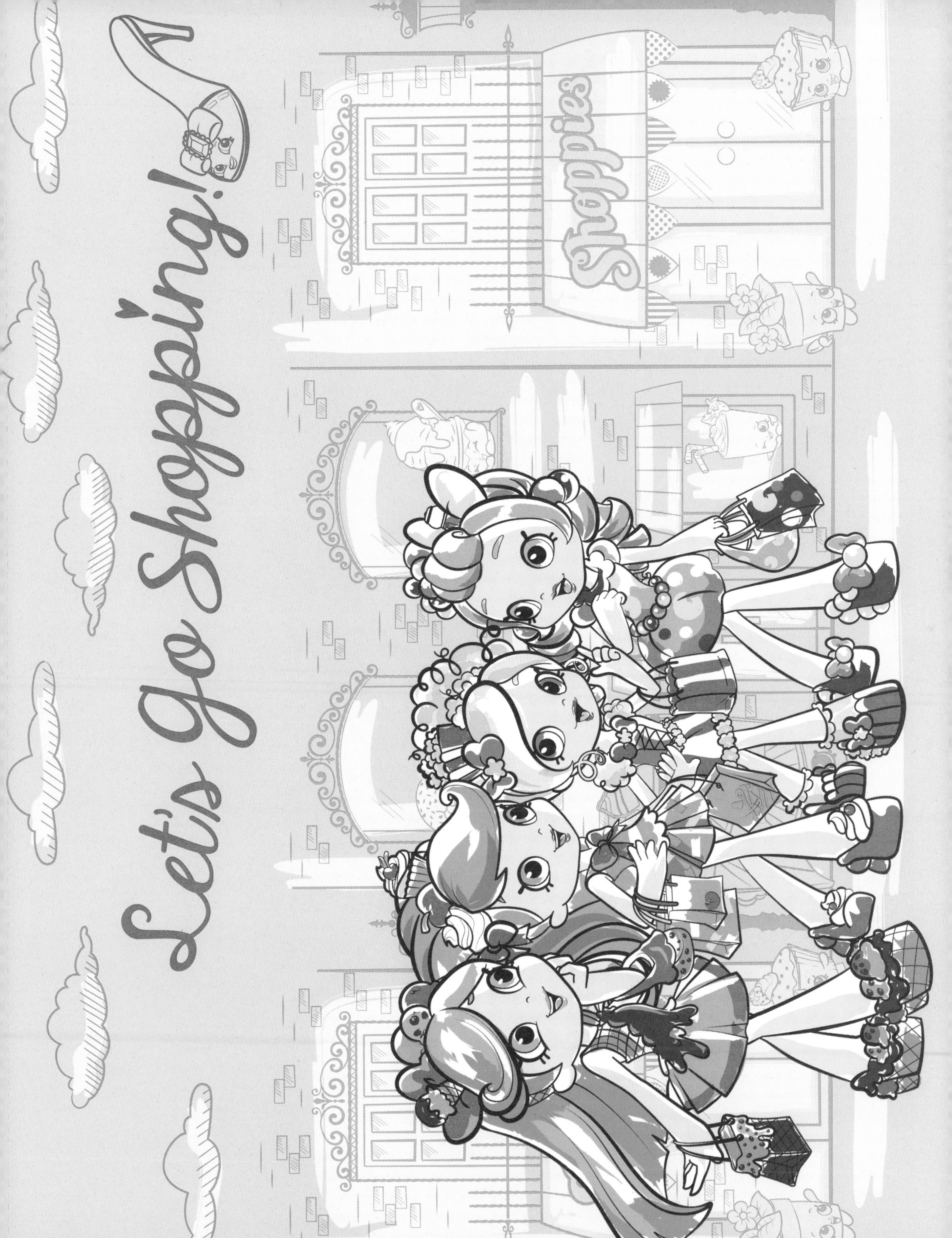
Let's Go Shopping!
Shoppies

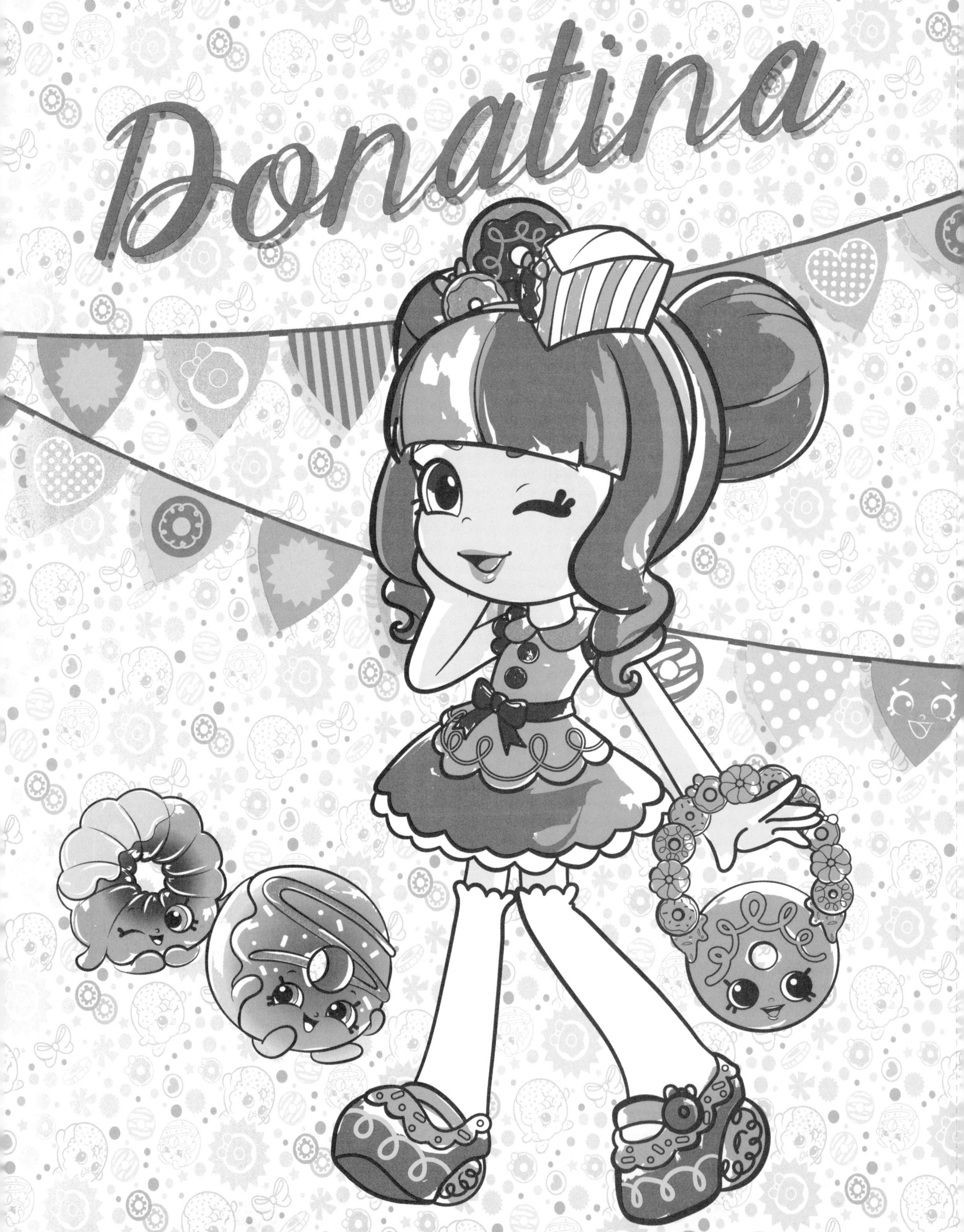
Donatina

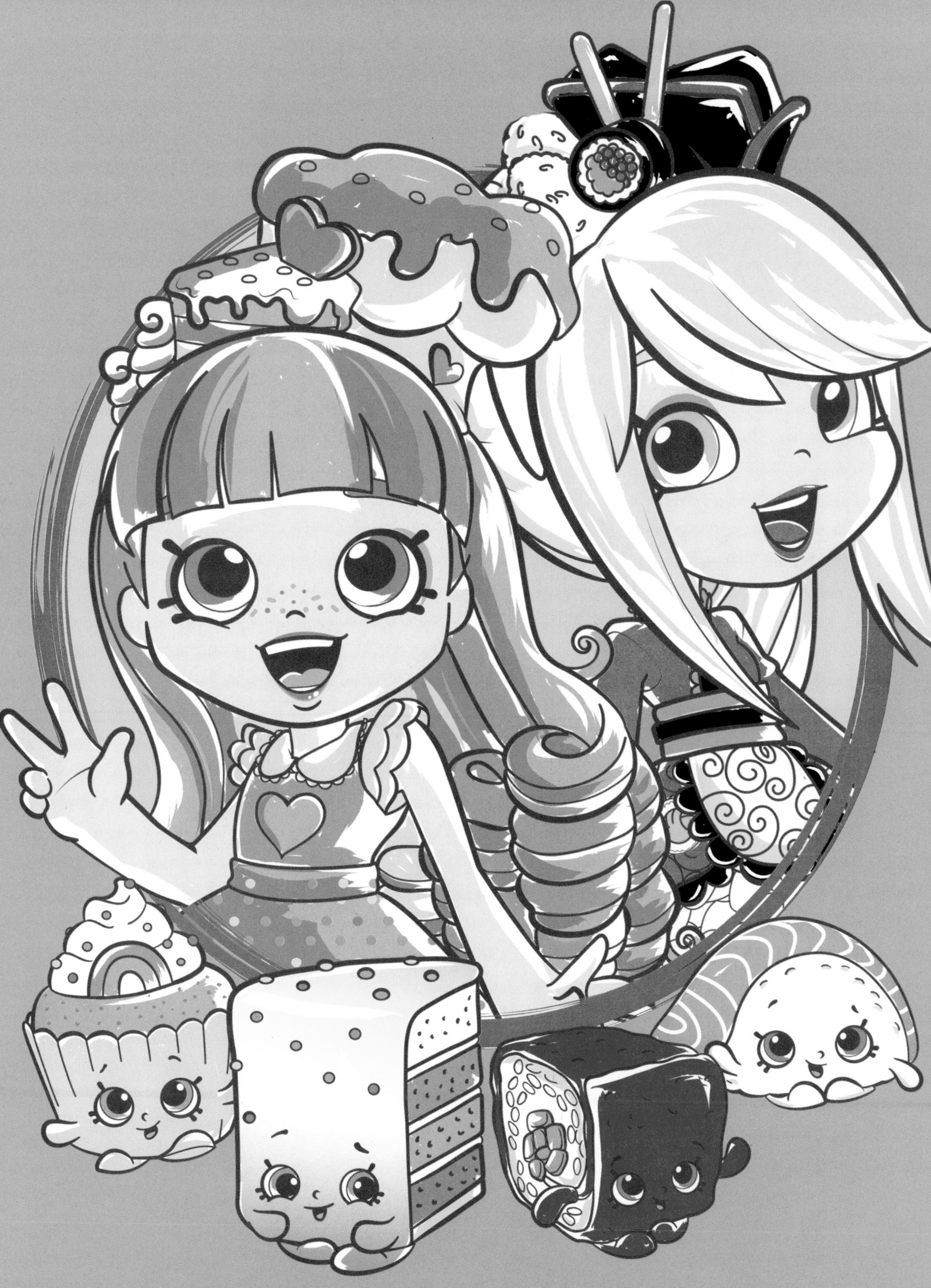

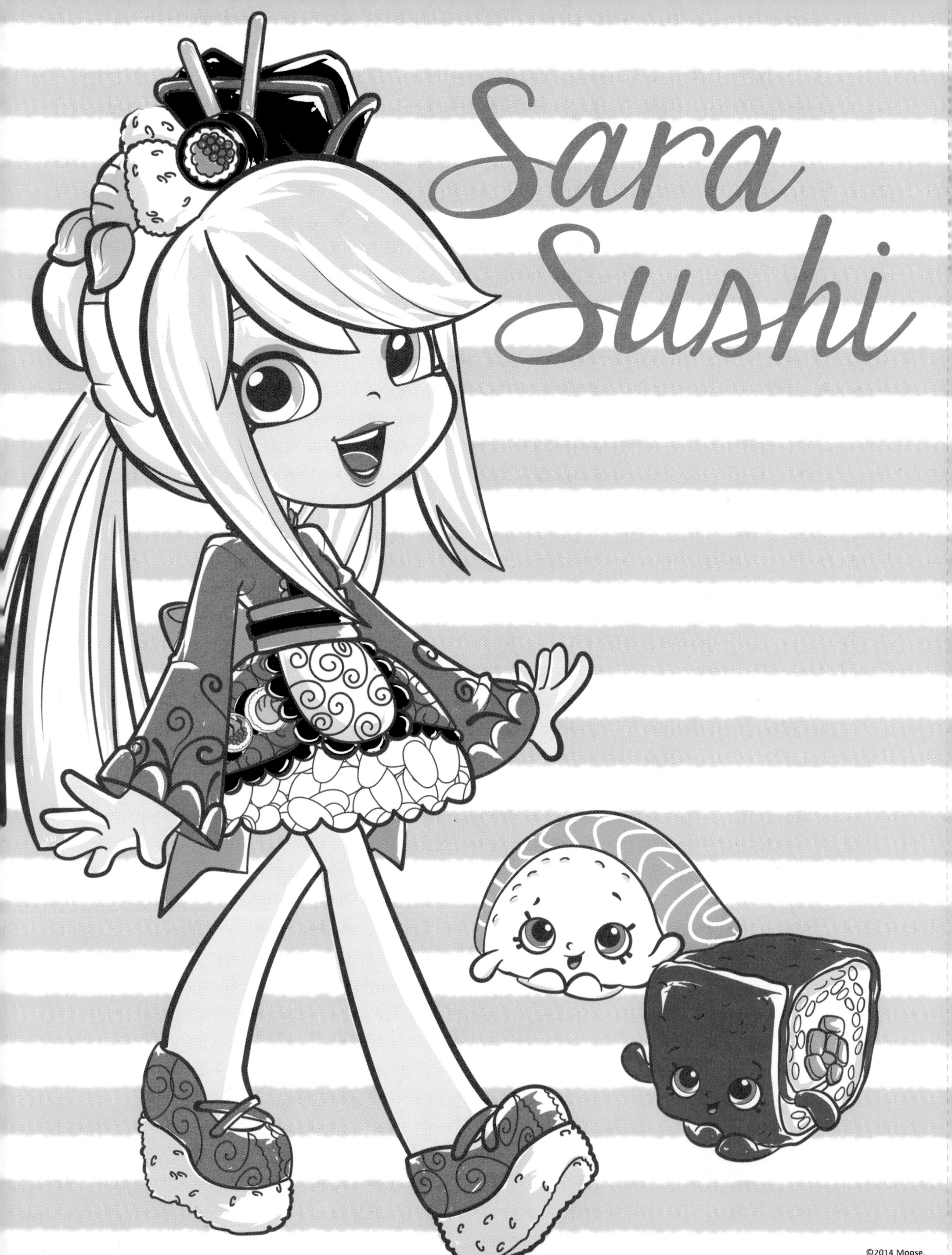
Sara
Sushi

RAINBOW KATE

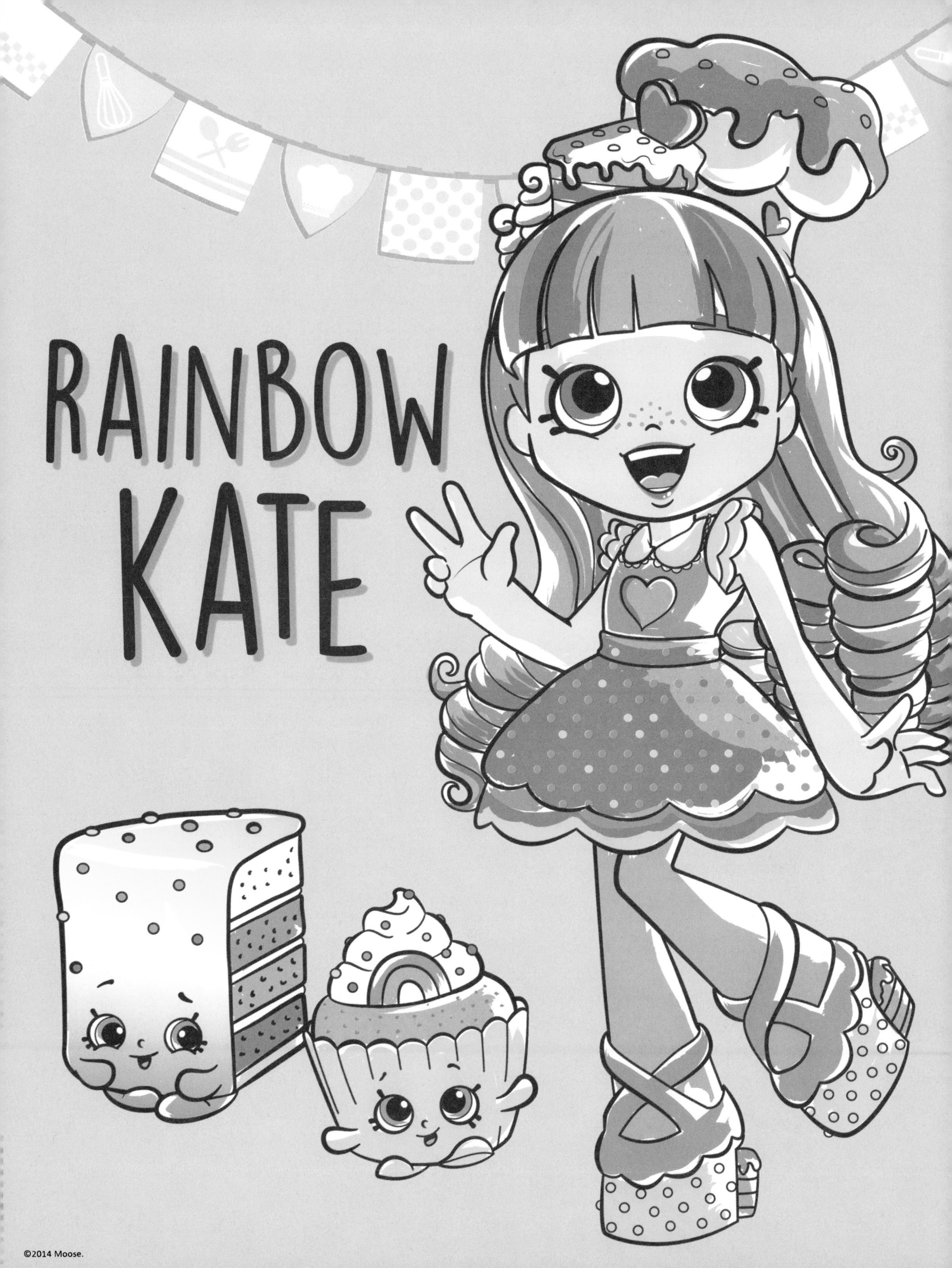

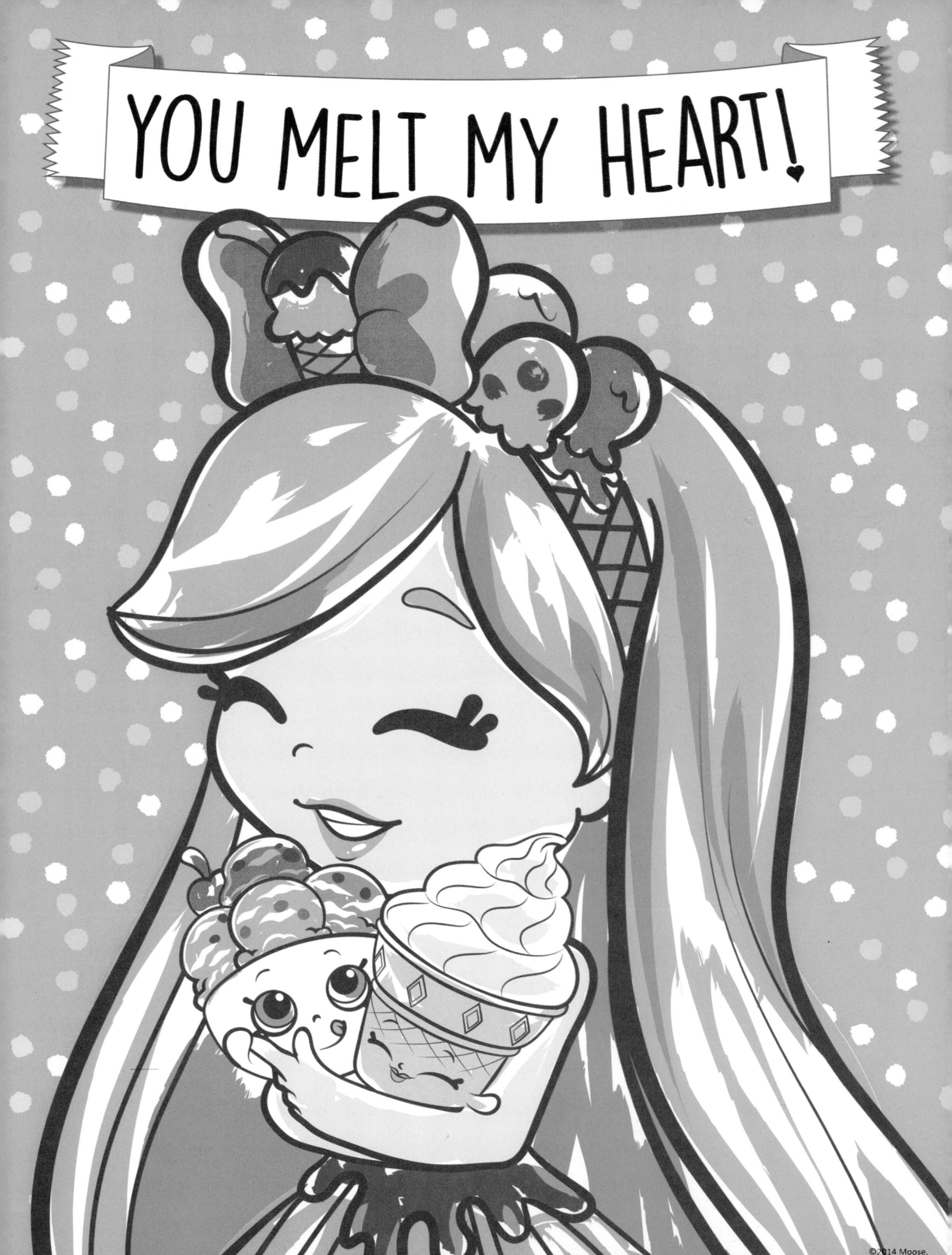
YOU MELT MY HEART!

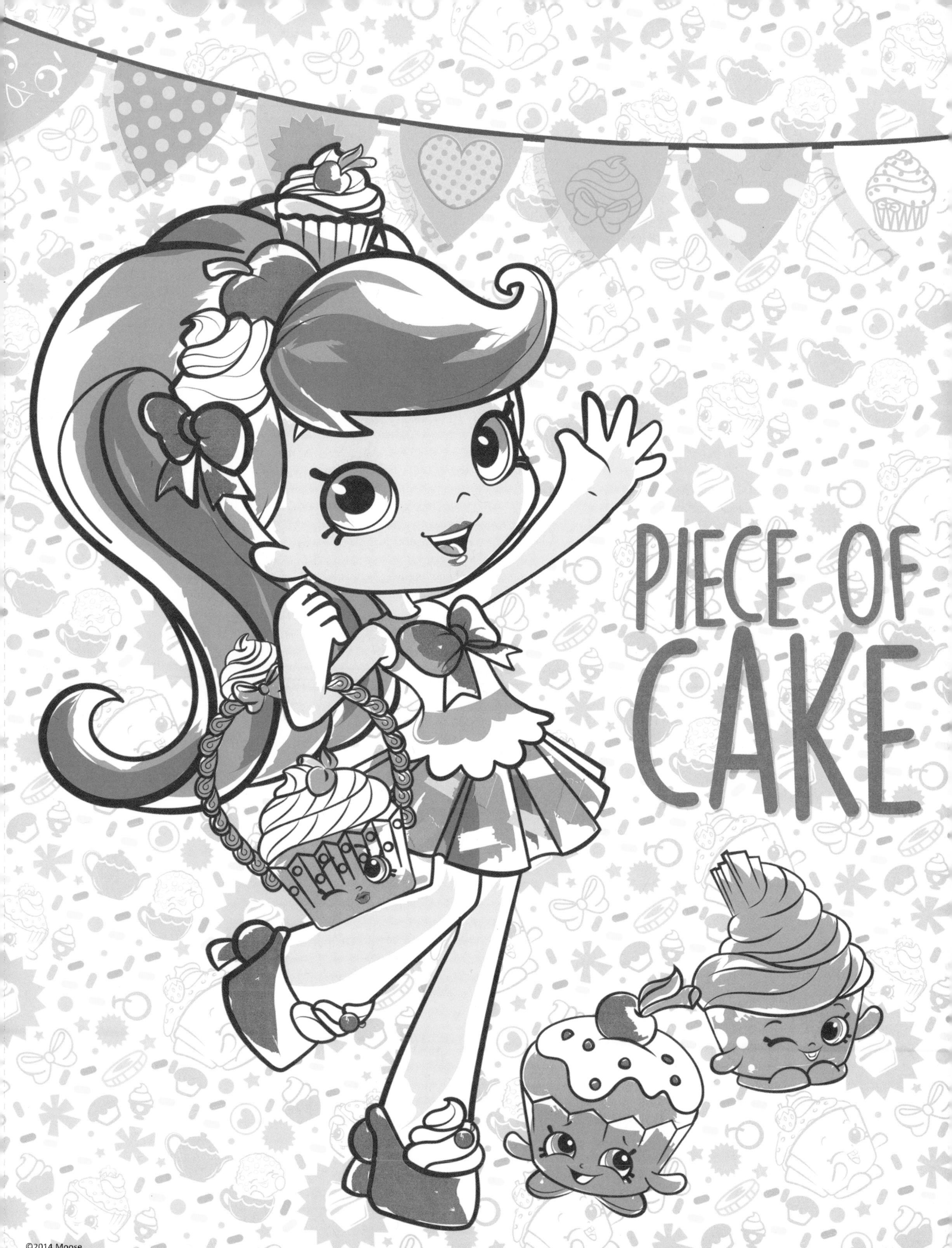
PIECE OF
CAKE

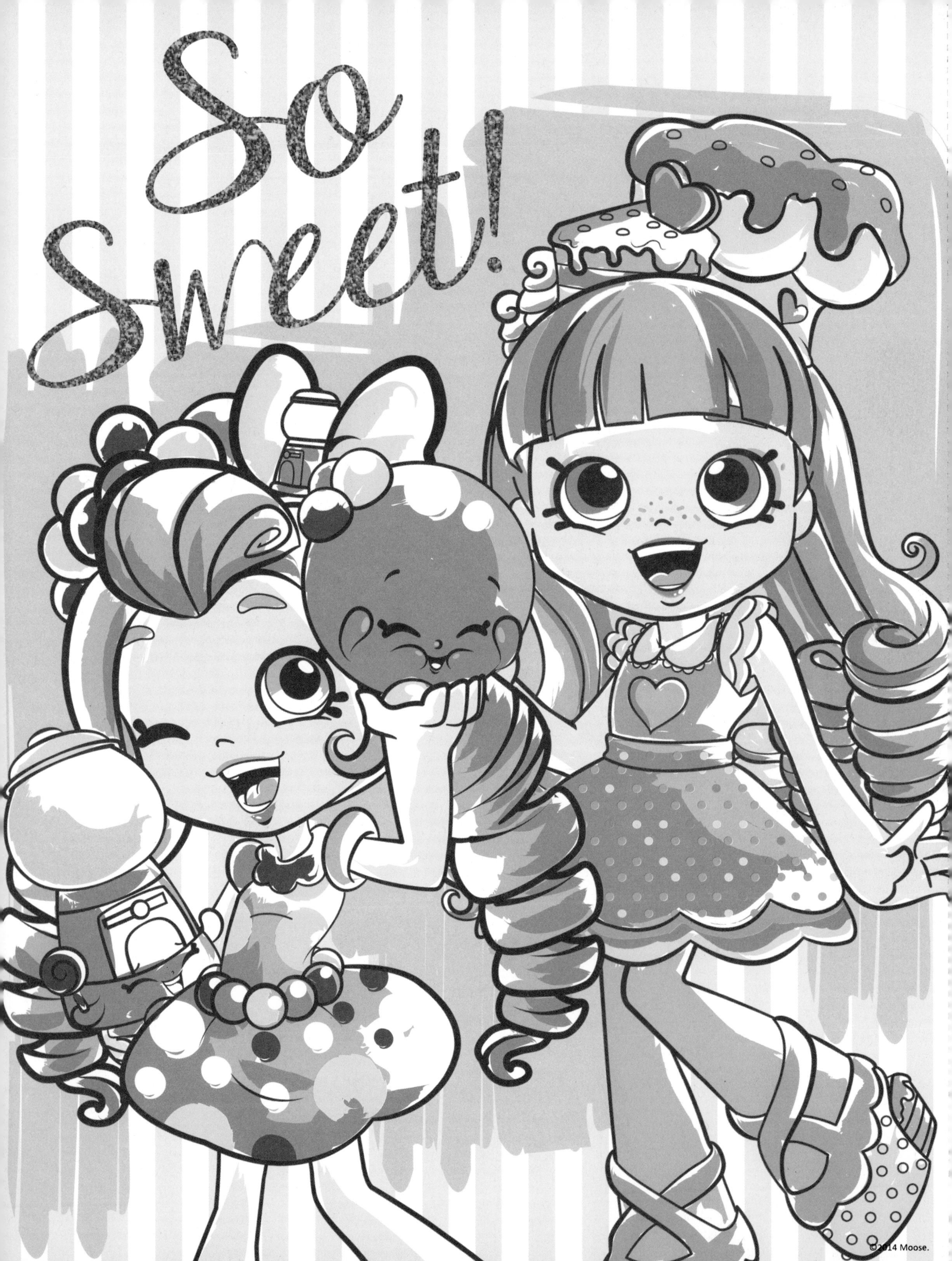
So
Sweet!

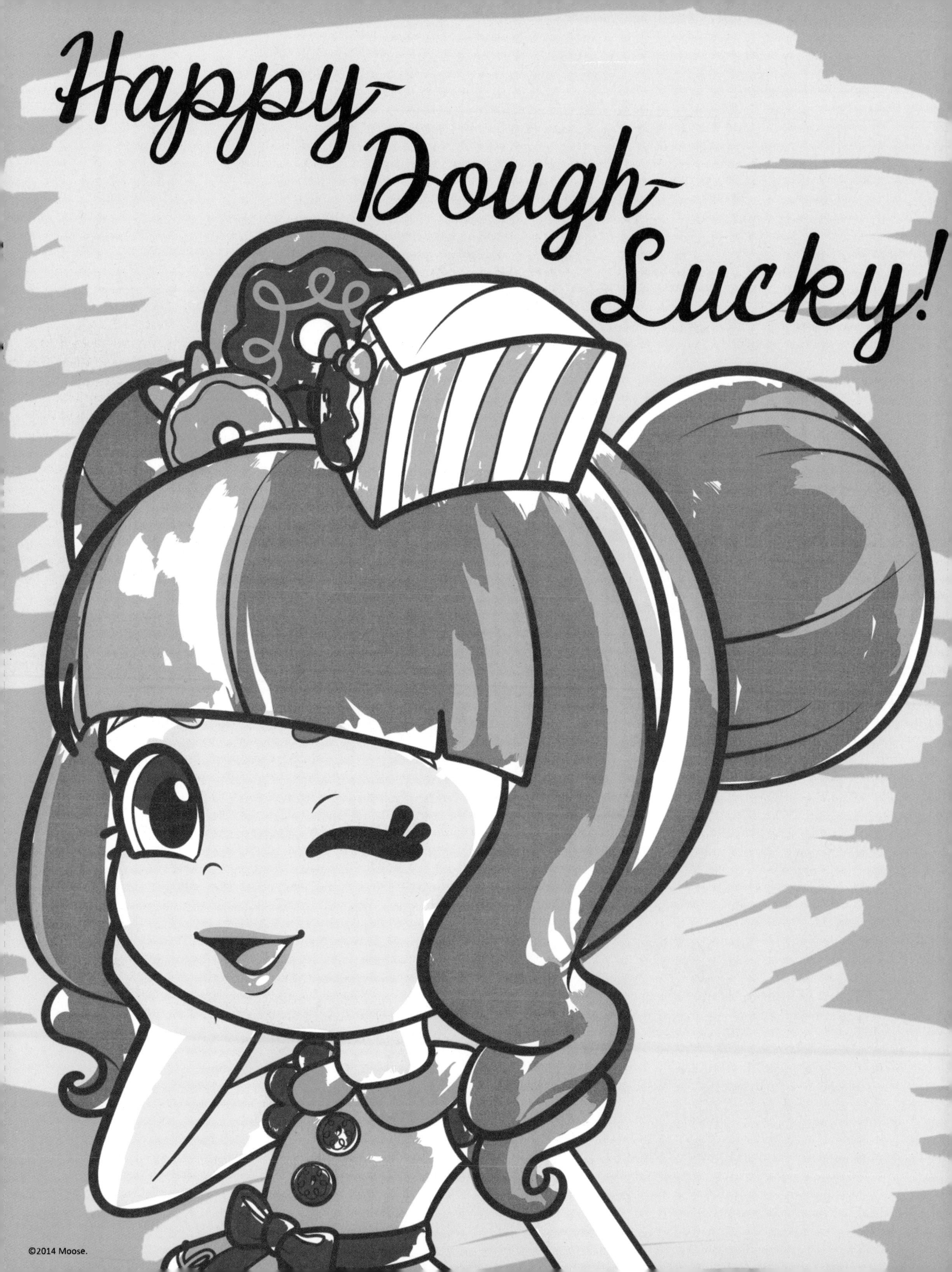
Happy-Dough-Lucky!

Friendship is Always in Style!

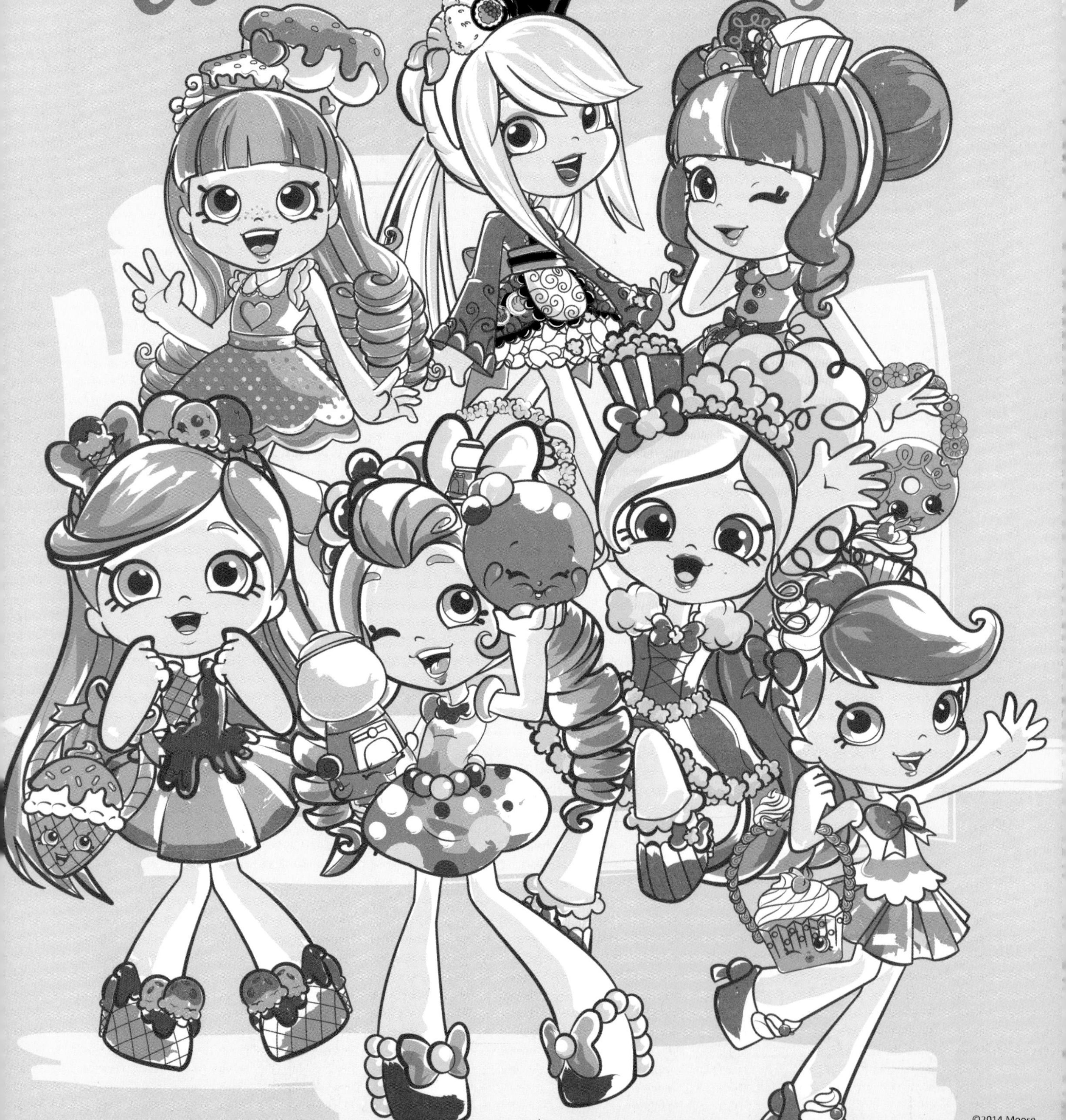